S rtsey
the Cat

by

Hilary Roper

Pattersand Press
info@pattersandpress.com | www.pattersandpress.com | www.hilaryroper.com

To Zoe o
Best wishes
Hilary Roper
2017.

Surtsey the Cat
Author and Illustrator Hilary Roper, 2013

ISBN 978-0-9575706-0-3

Pattersand Press
A British Product
Printing by Butler, Tanner & Dennis, Somerset, UK.

All the illustrations in this book have been hand painted.

For Isabelle

See if you can find the teddy bear in this book.

In the harbour, by the castle wall, there is a little cottage which overlooks the sea. A fisherman and his cat called Surtsey live in the cottage. They spend many happy hours mending the fisherman's nets on the quayside.

One bright sunny day, Surtsey asks the fisherman if he can go out to sea with him in his fishing boat.

"No!"

He replied. **"It is too dangerous.** I am sailing to Iceland where the shoals of fish swim, where the whales dive and splash in the cold, cold sea. It freezes there. You might slip off the edge of the boat and drown. Come on, let's go back to the cottage and have tea."

The very next morning the fisherman sets sail. The wind howls.

Swish

slosh

slash.

But Surtsey ignores the warning and climbs onto the boat. The fisherman has no idea Surtsey is there. The seagulls scream and screech trying to warn the fisherman but he cannot hear them. The little boat chugs out to sea.

Out comes the storm monster.
It hisses and wails as the little boat
rocks on the waves. The sea

foams

flicks

kicks

the little boat side to side.

The storm monster lashes out. The
storm tests the fisherman's skills
to the limit. Suddenly, a huge wave
smacks the boat and throws
Surtsey into the raging sea.

"Help!"

Cries Surtsey.

"I can't swim!"

Suddenly,

an angry shark swims by. Its teeth poke like spears. The shark wants Surtsey for its supper.

Surtsey falls further down to the bottom of the

deep
blue
sea.

How strange! Surtsey thinks. Here, sitting on the sandy, sea bed is a mermaid. She is busy. She is trying to teach the fish to swim in a line.

Surtsey offers to help her.

"Where have you come from?"
she asks. Surtsey replies,
    "I have lost my master and his fishing boat. I fell off the boat in the storm. He will be cross with me. I should not have climbed aboard."

"Look!"
she says. "I'm in a hurry. Come with me to the sea ball. Then I will help you find your master and his boat."

Hilary Roper

Surtsey and the mermaid swim to
the sea ball. The sea palace is guarded
by snapping lobsters. Their claws

crack

clack

click.

The sea king and queen dance with the mermaid and Surtsey.

"Tell me again," the mermaid asks, "where are you from?"

"I need to find my master's fishing boat," Surtsey replies. "I live with him in a tiny cottage in the harbour by the castle wall. He has no idea I am here. I am in trouble as I disobeyed him."

"Then I will help you," the mermaid says, "**but we must hurry**, before the storm monster stirs. The rain and wind will howl soon. We must find the fisherman's boat for you."

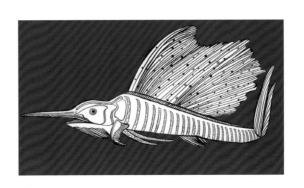

The mermaid and Surtsey swim as fast as they can. It is dangerous. The angry whales lash out with their tails.

"Look!"

Surtsey shouts. "There is my master's net. I help him mend the holes in his net. I can recognise those knots in the rope anywhere!"

"Quick!"

The mermaid shouts. "Climb into the net."

Surtsey clambers into the fisherman's net. The fish

slip

slop

slap.

The cod and the haddock slide about. The net is pulled up to the surface of the sea. Surtsey thanks the mermaid.

"One day, I will see you on the rocks where the otters play," Surtsey shouts happily.

The fisherman hauls his net into the boat. **He is shocked.** There before his very eyes, he sees Surtsey wet, bedraggled and sitting amongst the fish.

He is upset to see Surtsey cold and shivering. The fisherman finds a blanket to wrap around Surtsey. Surtsey meows happily.

The engines clang as the fisherman turns his boat around to sail home.

 "I will never break your rules again," Surtsey meows.

The fisherman can already see the harbour lights twinkle in the distance.

Back at home in the fisherman's cottage Surtsey is given fishy pie. They both warm themselves by the fire. The fisherman is secretly proud of Surtsey having been so brave.

"I'm sorry," Surtsey meows.

Purr Purr Purr.

"Next time, you must do as you are told," the fisherman says. "Sharks have **very** **big teeth**."

"I know!"

Surtsey meows.

Now, every time the fisherman goes out to sea, Surtsey is good and stays at home.

But just sometimes, he sneaks away across the slippery rocks to play with the silly otters. Sometimes the mermaid comes to play too.

"This is much more fun than going out to sea in a storm," Surtsey purrs.

Surtsey pretends to be an otter but the otters are only interested in one thing and one thing only ~

FISH!

The End

Sunset on Sea

The clouds in hues of mauves and purple,
Sneak before, a ruby bauble.
Streaks of freaky, yellow gold,
Tinsel orange glistening folds.
In shapes of dogs, cats and moles,
Dragon birds, giant souls.
Dolphins dive splish splosh splash,
Fishing boats sail back home fast,
Whales in circles make big waves,
Mermaids hide in secret caves.
Twilight sky, undisturbed
Fluffs by solemnly, unperturbed.